GHOST STORIES

OF

CHARLOTTE

AND

MECKLENBURG COUNTY

Ghost Stories of

Charlotte

and Mecklenburg County

Remnants of the Past in a New South

Stephanie Burt Williams

Winston-Salem, North Carolina

Copyright © 2003 by Stephanie Burt Williams

Printed in the United States of America

Library of Congress Control Number 2003102666

ISBN 1-878177-14-1

Bandit Books, Inc.
P.O. Box 11721
Winston-Salem, NC 27116-1721
(336) 785-7417

Distributed by John F. Blair, Publisher
(800) 222-9796
www.blairpub.com

Photographs by Stephanie Burt Williams, except as noted

Cover design by Holly Smith, bookskins.net

To the things that go bump in the night

and the people

who tell other people about them

Table of Contents

ACKNOWLEDGMENTS

I would like to thank the Charlotte-Mecklenburg Historic Landmarks Commission for their excellent web site, and Historic Rosedale for their contacts. Thanks also to all the people willing to talk to me about their experiences and answer my questions.

Davidson

Cornelius

Huntersville

Charlotte

Mint Hill

Matthews

Pineville

Mecklenburg County

INTRODUCTION

Charlotte and Mecklenburg County are for a lot of people a destination, a little placard on an airline terminal, but for my family and me this is home. Charlotte and its inhabitants often suffer from wanting to be something they are not. The Queen City gets compared to Atlanta, its poster "New South" city. Over the years I've heard Charlotte's night life, arts community, shopping, and general taste scoffed. But I think one thing that Charlotte *is* missing is its own collection of ghost stories.

I have been reading ghost stories since at least junior high school and have been especially interested in those of local origin. Sure, I watch those Discovery Channel specials on the ghosts of English castles, but it is the specials on Charleston and New Orleans that get me to bring out the popcorn and dim the lights.

I don't think I am an anomaly in this sense. We like to hear things about the places we visit, or find out more about what we think we already know; I don't know when or if I'll ever get to visit the haunted castles of England, but I've been to Savannah and New Orleans and will most likely visit again. These are southern places, just down the road, and still a little part of "me." There is something fascinating about the secrets behind some building or city, and if we know those secrets, we feel in a small sense that we can begin to claim that place as ours.

Ghost stories are the best secrets. Many people don't even like to discuss them, and those that do often take a delicious relish in telling the tales under their breath or behind closed doors. And that is one thing that I think Charlotte and the people who visit it don't realize it has–secrets. Charlotte seems transparent, a city obviously built on business with shiny new buildings, shiny new subdivisions surrounding every cul-de-sac, and plenty of shiny new people just moved from someplace else. Mecklenburg County seems easy to understand. But Charlotte, the new south city, sometimes forgets its history, often knocking down and paving over the past.

Yet, if you look under the surface or just around the corner, the past is still here, still evident. It's in the stories we tell each other about the places we live and work. Ghost stories are the closest we can come to actually experiencing the past. You've perhaps scraped a layer of paint off a wall or mantelpiece only to reveal a color beneath that is surprising. Who decided on this color? you may think. Who lived here before me?

Ghost stories give us a chance to fill in those blanks. Instead of knowing simply the names and years associated with the house, often ghosts have personalities–mischievous or sad or always wanting to turn down the thermostat. These are small, human things that fill out existence. The fact that a ghost bridges the gap between past and present means those that come in contact somehow do as well–and that the past isn't forgotten.

We tend to think of history as names and dates—something that we've often heard is "dry" or "boring," but of course history is learning about ourselves. It is about learning why we call a street something or what used to be there before the corner Eckerd's or how the person in your house lived in the same space but in a different way. We might forget the details, like last names or dates, and some of the remaining details can be subject to change with the telling, but the essence is there—"something happened here."

And if the details do get changed, that educates us about the tellers of these tales, and the ones that experience the ghosts firsthand. We learn about each other through conversation, what we remember, and what we forget. A ghost story is easy to remember.

So now Charlotte has secrets, although of course it always did. These are places that you know, places that in many cases you can visit. Most of these locations are businesses because business is what has preserved what is left of Charlotte's physical history. And the ghosts run the gamut from Revolutionary War hero to a lonely caterer, a diversity that reflects Charlotte well. So begin to claim this place as ours—it is after all—for we know some of its secrets.

HOPEWELL PRESBYTERIAN CHURCH
GHOST RIDER

Hopewell Presbyterian Church has been a fixture in Mecklenburg County since before the American Revolution. Located on Beatties Ford Road right across the street from the entrance to Latta Plantation Park, it was first incorporated in the 1760s, meeting in a simple log structure. The brick building was built around 1830 and is a wonderful example of the federal style of church. This was the place of worship for the influential planters in the northern part of the county, including the Alexander, Torrence, Davidson, and Latta families (take note—check other chapters to see these names again!) However, it is not the impressive church itself that lends us a ghostly encounter, but the cemetery, always a classic setting for a supernatural tale.

If ever in this part of the county, stop and visit the cemetery. It's a wonderful place, with its family plots and soapstone markers that look as good today as when they were carved at the beginning of the nineteenth century. The whole area is enclosed with a low wall of river stone, and large trees shade part of the property. Here are buried many of the most prominent of the early inhabitants of this region, including General William Davidson.

Hopewell Presbyterian Church, the place of worship and final resting place for many of Mecklenburg County's most prominent citizens

General Davidson led the fight to arrest the stampede of Major General Lord Charles Cornwallis' British army into this territory during the American Revolution. On February 1, 1781, Davidson rode out on his impressive steed to lead his troops into the Battle of Cowan's Ford, fought at a site only minutes by car from Hopewell Presbyterian Church, at the edge of Lincoln and Mecklenburg Counties. General Davidson became the first fatality of the battle. The British subsequently stripped off his clothing, either for intelligence gathering or to undermine American morale, and left his naked corpse lying on the ground.

Under cloak of darkness that very night, Davidson's loyal men spirited his body away from the battlefield to Hopewell's cemetery for burial. It is easy to imagine his troops taking pains that this last act for their general, although hurried, be honorable and right. His grieving widow secretly attended the quick service.

There was much controversy over the years as to whether Davidson was actually buried in the cemetery, since the service had been so secret, but recently infrared imaging has proven that there is a body under the general's marker. Nevertheless, it seems as if Davidson himself wishes to assure his troops of his proper, if hasty, burial.

On the night of February 1st each year the general takes his horse for a ride through the cemetery. The ghost rider appears out of the air to cross silently over the existing gravestones. He lifts his saber to hearten his troops for battle, before he disappears into the mist.

Reverend Jeff Lowrance, the pastor of Hopewell Presbyterian, lives in the manse directly across from the cemetery. Being an aficionado of history himself, Reverend Lowrance related the tale to his two daughters, whose bedrooms look out onto the grave-yard. "You thought they forgot about it," he said, smiling, "but when they were little, as February 1st approached, they would worry about seeing the general ride by their window. They would not look out for fear of seeing him, and laid awake worrying about it." Lowrance has never seen the general galloping across the cemetery, but he says that many people plan to "camp out" on that night. Most simply forget to.

Originally, there was a brick structure called a "bridge" over the grave as a marker to the general. Later it was removed and a new, more traditional marker installed. Nevertheless, the marker is easy to find, for the church has mapped out the graveyard with a named key for each of its inhabitants.

It seems that General Davidson has not forgotten that fateful day. Driving past Hopewell on foggy winter nights, with the low stone wall glowing slightly from the reflected street light, it's easy to think you hear the hooves of a horse, clanking on top of the tilted gravestones.

The gravestone of General William Lee Davidson

ANTIQUE KINGDOM

THE OLD BOARDING HOUSE

"I am not one to believe in ghosts. The other night when I woke up and saw two women standing by my bed, I never thought they were ghosts. I thought maybe that I had died."

These are the words of Phillip Highsmith, the owner, along with his son Steve, of Antique Kingdom on Central Avenue in Charlotte. A retired physics professor now in his second profession as an antiques dealer, Mr. Highsmith fancies himself a logical man who doesn't believe in such rubbish as ghosts. This is a hard task, especially considering the business he now owns. Although he and his son do not believe in them, they have names for their ghosts.

The building that is Antique Kingdom has seen the flux of Charlotte's change. Built circa 1900, it originally served as a boarding house for those staying in Charlotte. Many Southern Bell employees stayed here over the years when business called them into town, as well as the usual traveling salesman and those sightseeing from the country. The building sat, and still sits, on the edge of downtown, acting as a sort of segue into Charlotte's first suburbs, including Elizabeth and Plaza-Midwood.

But the boarding house was not all warm meals in the dining room or comfortable beds. It was well known as a place where one could "get a nip" as it were, for it served as home base to a bootlegging operation that existed for a number of years. In fact, traditional North Carolina "moonshine" was made here and many times sold in the house, right under the noses of its more law-abiding guests.

Also, the story goes that not too many years ago, a married couple lived in the house. They were not happy and often had loud fights. The woman passed away, and her husband sent her to a mortuary to be buried, but never paid the bill. She laid in state for a whole month until finally the county had to cremate her and cite the husband. So even at her death he wasn't able to release his grudge.

These tales lend a sinister glow to the house. Its many windows look out onto Central Avenue, and its gables and wide front porch are still intact after all these years. And although no one is allowed in after business hours here, you might just see someone peeking back at you from an upstairs window.

When Phillip and Steve first purchased the property and began doing some renovations on it, many of the workmen, as well as the owners themselves, noticed a distinct vibration about the house, even a sort of audible humming. Phillip assumed it was a roadway passing so close, but never got a satisfactory explanation. After working one morning, a plumber refused to work in the house any longer since "it gave him the creeps and he wasn't going to be alone" in there anymore.

A few months later the vibration stopped, but then they noticed other strange occurrences in the house. First, the front door started popping open on a regular basis. It is a heavy, wooden door with an intricate latch that cannot easily be blown open, yet this happens. The door opens when the store is quiet and also when there are people about; it does not matter. Phillip asserts that it opens anywhere from once a month to once a week.

Antique Kingdom

"When it happens, I just say, 'Gertrude or Myrtle, I can't keep it cool in here if you keep opening the door,'" he explained. And then he closes the door and it doesn't open again for a while. When asked why he chose those names to address the door, he said they "just sounded right."

The front door of Antique Kingdom often opens of its own accord.

Steve does not claim that he has seen anything; nevertheless, he has an elaborate system of turning off the lights at night on the upper two floors. As to his reason for this system, he just says that he doesn't want to be up there in the dark.

When the author went to interview the Highsmiths for this story, it was neither dark nor night, but a sunny summer morning. Upon walking upstairs, while glancing in one particular room, as she is interested in antiques, suddenly the hair on the back of her neck stood up and she got a horrible case of the chills. Then, ever so slightly, something touched the back of her neck. Later as she recounted the story to the Highsmiths, they refused to return upstairs with her. "We really don't go up there unless we have to," Steve explained.

Still, one evening in May 2002 something definite happened to Phillip, and he was not upstairs. After a long day of inventory, he was sleeping in the office, which once was a kitchen for the boarding house. In the middle of the night he woke up, and about three feet from him stood a woman and a teenaged girl. He recalled their dress as "old fashioned, maybe from the twenties, but like they were going to a wedding or something. I asked, 'What are you doing here?' I didn't recognize them, but they gave me, I thought, a look that said 'come with us,' so I got up. As soon as I got up, they started to disappear slowly, from the center out, almost like molecules breaking apart. I wasn't scared, but had a sense of peace." Phillip said there was no light in the room except for the faint glow from a streetlight outside the window, yet he could see them clearly.

After all of this, the Highsmiths still are reluctant to call what they have "ghosts."

"We hear people walking upstairs when no one is there all the time," Steve said as he stood at the front desk and gestured toward the ceiling. "I don't really think about it that much—it happens so often." Steve and Phillip assert that those footsteps are not customers; they're just not ghosts.

THE MANOR THEATRE

ALL DRESSED UP AND NOWHERE TO GO

The lights are down low, you're reclining into a plush chair, and images are flickering on a screen before you. We've all been there, that great feeling of relaxation while watching a movie. No other place in Charlotte holds quite the same mystique for this feeling as the Manor Theatre on Providence Road. Yes, there are theaters that show more movies, and ones that have stadium seating, but where else can you find old fashioned charm and the possibility of a ghost taking a seat beside you during the show?

Built in 1947, the Manor was hailed as the most beautiful in Charlotte (albeit by its own advertising), but it remains today as the grand duchess of theaters. Throughout the years it has realized its tie to the community with varied events such as the giving away of live chicks around Easter, or the special matinees for children during the summer. Now it serves as the venue for the Charlotte Film Society, consistently offering independent and foreign films. Still, with all the joy and entertainment the movie theater brings, it is not without its sadness.

One of the early managers of the Manor in 1947 decided to end it all. He committed suicide at home. Since that time the manager has appeared on a regular basis around the theater.

Above: The Manor Theatre

Below: Often while employees are cleaning up at night, they
hear sweeping in the lobby or the stairwell above them.

Always dressed impeccably in a dinner jacket, the nightly uniform for his position, he appears in the theater, usually late at in the evening. Many witnesses attest that they've seen, after the doors were locked, a white-haired man in the Manor. Upon asking, "Can I help you?" the man simply disappears. He looks totally real and solid, thus fooling the employees, who often wonder how he got in.

Employees have also seen him in the projection booth. Usually he is sweeping in that area. Recently during the Thursday night preview of a new movie, one of the employees heard sweeping. Wondering who could be cleaning at that hour, he leaned out of the projection booth to see who it was. About that time he felt a bump on his foot that was sticking out into the hallway. It was just as if someone had run a push broom against his foot. Then the sweeping sound continued past him, all the way down the corridor. I doubt the employee paid much attention to the movie after that.

However, the suicidal manager is not the only spirit that lurks about the place. Ann Kesiah, a relief manager who has been with the Manor for many years, says that while she's downstairs in her office she often hears the sound of a woman's high heels clicking toward the bathroom. A medium who was there to see a movie reported to one of the employees that she got a strong impression in the women's powder room of a lady named Rose.

One night Kesiah heard one of her employees, Tracy Kelly, scream from the upstairs bathroom. As she dashed up the steps to investigate, Kesiah felt a cold pass by her, a cold that was unlike any other she had experienced. She continued up to help the

The upstairs gallery of the Manor Theatre, where one can
hear the echoes of ghostly footsteps of a woman in high heels

clearly shaken Kelly, who explained, "While I was in the bathroom, someone hit the wall very hard. They were in the powder
room." The only way out of that room was down the stairs, and
Kesiah had seen nothing when she ran up to see what was
wrong–though she had felt something. Kelly, understandably,
took the rest of the evening off.

As the 21st century began the Manor was in grave danger of
closing, put out of the market by multiplexes in the suburbs. But
with the Charlotte Film Society and the citizens who rallied
around it in support for an independent venue, the Manor seems
destined to spend many more years providing a wonderful place
to see a flick. And if you see a man in a dinner jacket walk down
the aisle, slide over a little to give more room for the seat beside
you. You never know, he just might bring you some free popcorn.

The ladies' powder room, where a medium sensed a spirit
named Rose, and an employee had a more definitive experience

Cedar Grove

CEDAR GROVE

A FAMILY ROOTED IN TIME

Ghostly lights, horse hooves, the sound of people upstairs. It's not hard to believe when you round the bend on Gilead Road and Cedar Grove comes into view. With its elegant, columned house, and the Hugh Torrence House and Store sitting just beside it, it is easy to imagine many generations spending their lives here—and some sticking around to see what happens next.

Belle Banks, mistress of this grand old house, has spent many years renovating it and preserving it for the future. Her late husband, Dick Banks, was a direct descendent of the Torrence family who built the house and store beside it. The family has resided in Mecklenburg County since the early days of the nation. Legend says that Hugh Torrence came to this country as an indentured servant. He first settled in Pennsylvania, and then moved to Mecklenburg County, where it did not take him long to prosper.

James Torrence built Cedar Grove in 1831 directly beside his father's store. The family's land once stretched over one thousand acres. The cotton plantation, which included a sawmill, gristmill, and store, was a virtual town in itself that drew the rest of the county to it for the goods and services it provided. James

Torrence married three times, and although it is not known how many slaves he owned, at the time of his death he left sixty-five to his widow.

Since the house is still owned by the original family, and since this family and the property have been prominent in the area for so long, the old plantation has taken on mythical proportions. For many years Belle Banks brought children in on Halloween to sit at the base of the three-story spiral staircase. There she told them ghost stories. Their parents often strained to glimpse the beauty of the interior of the house, including the twenty-foot ceilings and exquisite woodwork.

It was around this annual event that Banks' first experience with the paranormal occurred. A lively woman with a sparkle in her eye, she is not one that is easily spooked. On the other hand, she enjoys a good laugh, and explains this story away by saying it was a trick of shadow, although she has seen this many times.

The story goes that there was a woman murdered at the store next door, back in the days when it was operational. Her name was lost to time, but she is not forgotten. As if often the case with those taken hastily from life, she apparently is stuck in this realm, and can be seen, candle in hand, searching for something around the store at night. Perhaps she still wants the wares she wished to purchase, or perhaps she is looking for her assailant. No matter the reason, she is not at rest, "for there is always a flickering over there at night," Banks said. "I used to take the church kids over there at night and let them look. Sure enough, we would see a light flickering." A small light like the flame of a candle roams about the property, its cause unknown.

One of the rooms at Cedar Grove

Another unseen presence made itself known to Banks, and this time she was not as quick to dismiss it. She sat alone, reading, in the parlor downstairs one morning, around two a.m. Her children were asleep and her husband was away on business. She recalled, "I distinctly heard the sound of someone pushing heavy furniture across the attic." It was a stormy night, yet having weathered many a storm in the house, Banks knew that these sounds weren't normal. "I didn't go up there, and when Dick got home, I told him what I had heard. He said, 'Belle, that was just the wind.'" She said that she responded, "Dick, give me some credit as an intelligent woman. I know what the wind sounds like and that was not it." The attic, filled with books and papers from two centuries of the family's history, is foreboding enough in the daytime. There are few who would venture up after dark, much less under those circumstances.

Banks states that only occasionally has she felt a presence around when no one could be seen. Otherwise she has a great feeling about her home. "Many people have told me they sense a good feeling about the house, a strong feeling of good vibes, and I sense this myself," she said with a smile. "I am family. I am supposed to be here."

However one guest, Lynn Beard, someone Banks called "not a fanciful man," said he often told her of his strange experiences in the house. A rocking chair would start rocking when he was in the room with it, and there was a door that would not stay closed. "He told me too that often something would pull the bedcovers off him while he was sleeping." Let's just say it would only take one time for this to happen to the writer. She wouldn't stay any longer for this to happen "often!"

On certain nights, if you drive around that bend, a fog bank will have settled around the house and grounds. On such nights some have heard phantom horse hooves on a wooden bridge just past the house, as if someone were making their way after all this time to the store or to the house itself possibly for a family visit.

Probably the most famous of all of Cedar Grove's ghosts is the spirit of Great Uncle John Torrence, who took over his outfit when his commanding officer was killed in a Civil War battle. He is often seen at an upstairs window, facing the store in full Confederate uniform, calling for his dog, Belle (yes, ironic, but only a coincidence). Ike Graham, now deceased, was a descendent of the slaves of the plantation, and used to tell stories of the "haints"

Views of the impressive spiral staircase at Cedar Grove

about the place, especially Uncle John. He said that the figure looked like a real person, not faint or transparent, standing at the window, calling his dog around dusk.

Although his ghost is not seen anymore, people have reported hearing him coming down the spiral staircase. His peg leg makes a distinct sound on each step. Or was that just a trick for the youngsters at Halloween? Fact and fiction weave together effortlessly at Cedar Grove, making it not only the stuff of legend, but also one of the few survivors of Mecklenburg's planter past.

MAGIC MAZE

HOME OF THE LADY IN GRAY

At the corner of Euclid and East Boulevard stand two houses, tall and narrow in dark red brick, their facades covered by the screen of a tree or two. If you drive down East Boulevard, the one with all the costumes in the front yard and on the porch is known as Magic Maze costume shop. It is here that strange things just keep happening.

This house seems to attract "the unusual." It is now, and has been for some years, filled literally to capacity, floor to ceiling, with clothing of all types. Crammed into corners, the clothes hang in a loose categorization by time period. Of course, during the Halloween season many customers squeeze by racks to sift through gloves and hats and the occasional lei to find the perfect costume. But it is in the quiet times, early in the morning or late in the evening, when other guests feel more at home to rummage through the place.

Built as part of Dilworth, the first suburb of Charlotte, the building on East Boulevard was first a private residence. In 1916 John and Lillie Mae Wilkes lived there. They were typical middle-class people, he a traveling salesman, she a homemaker. During the 1930s the house went through a conversion into

Brumfield Photography Studio, where for a number of years Charlotte area high school seniors posed for pictures. Later the building served as a boarding house. Amazingly enough, one of the current residents boarded there when he first moved to Charlotte. Next the building became what neighborhood residents called "a drag queen bordello." Finally it became what it is now—a costume shop.

Robyn Query owns the costume shop and lives in the apartment above it. She loves and collects vintage clothing. Her shop is a virtual history tour of clothing from the twentieth century—including of course the required Bo Peep and M&M Man costumes. Robyn seems a quirky and creative individual, yes, but not one that is prone to imaginations. She simply accepts the world with all its eccentricities. So it was no surprise when one evening a few years ago, as she sat with a group of friends in her living room, someone asked, "Who's that?" They pointed to a woman walking by the door on her way down the steps.

"Everybody there saw it," Query said. "There were about seven of us, and I explained to them that that was the Lady in Gray."

Query is quite familiar with the Lady in Gray, who looks like a blurred black and white photograph, and always shows up around the attic door. She comes out of the attic and disappears after walking a few steps. She usually shows up between dusk and eight p.m., but on occasion Query has walked out of her bedroom in the middle of the night to go to the restroom, and "bumped" into the Lady in Gray.

Front view of Magic Maze

"I'm half asleep, and so I say, 'I'm sorry,' before realizing what just happened."

No matter when the Lady appears, she is always dressed in the same thing—a dark charcoal gray dress with a high collar and long skirts, and her hair is done up like a Gibson girl.

"She never makes it down to the first landing," Query said. "She always disappears after a couple of steps."

But it seems that that is not the only sometime visitor. Christina McDonald, an employee at the Magic Maze for over six years, has encountered some "things" on the bottom floor among the costumes, as well as in the apartment upstairs. "I saw the racks moving in the back room and thought it was the cat walking across the hangers," McDonald said. "I then noticed the cat was beside me, and the rack was still moving, so I leaned in closer, walking toward a part of the costumes. What I saw was a pair of eyes surrounded by gray curly hair, and I was mesmerized. The eyes were illuminated and kind of scary looking, but I wasn't afraid." McDonald turned to go get someone else, and by the time they returned, the "thing" was gone.

McDonald seems to be a target for the spirits in the house. She hears noises that sound like customers in the store when there are none, and sometimes even hears people calling her name. She also came upon what she thinks was the spirit of a child. In that same back room, there is a large freestanding mirror. McDonald, while working there, saw the mirror fog up as if a small child had breathed on it. As she ran out of the room, she heard behind her a child laughing.

And then upstairs, one evening McDonald saw someone appear on the steps. It was not the Lady in Gray, but another woman dressed in a yellow party dress. When McDonald noticed her, the woman looked back over her shoulder and smiled. "She was very graceful and elegant, and had auburn hair. Her dress was very full."

Upon visiting the Magic Maze, the author felt a couple of cold spots—telltale signs of ghosts—in the house. The cold could have come from her imagination after the number of stories she'd heard. Or it could have come from something beyond the explainable.

Does a long and varied history explain all of this activity in the building, or is there something more? McDonald said, "A lot of the costumes that we have, we get from families of people who have just died." Query will receive a call, and go over and clean out closets, bringing back everything from shoes to dresses. Perhaps the deceased people don't wish to give up their clothing. After all, what is more personal than your favorite dress or hat?

Or could the Lady in Gray be Lillie Mae, still keeping her house? Next time you visit, try calling her name—and see what happens.

Delectables by Holly, home to the ghost called Alice

DELECTABLES BY HOLLY
AND SOMETHING CLASSIC CATERING

ALICE STILL LIVES THERE

On the corner of 5th and Independence, right beside the famous blues club, the Double Door, sits a little bungalow. Aside from the imaginative paint job, which is a whimsical garden, there is nothing outstanding about the structure. It is one of many Charlotte bungalows, an architectural style that the city fell in love with in the 1920s and still builds a lot of today. This particular bungalow was built around the 1940s. It has housed a catering business, although not the same one, since the sixties.

Three caterers have occupied the building: Alice's Catering, Something Classic, and currently Delectables by Holly. The fact that this building, located in an area of town that has seen many changes, has had the same use for so long is quite rare. But even more rare are the things that happen in this little place.

When Jill Markus, owner of Something Classic Catering, moved in in the late eighties, Alice still lived upstairs as she had the entire time she operated her business. An elderly lady who seemed somewhat lost now that she no longer worked, Alice was thrilled that catering would continue from this location. "We were doing a lot of renovations, and she lived there about a month,"

Markus recalled. "One day, Alice came and told us that she had found another apartment and seemed happy about it. Five days after she left, she passed away. It was then that things started happening."

Markus immediately felt that there was a presence in the house. It looked after her and her employees, but nevertheless, that presence wanted to make itself known. Markus and several of her employees often saw something move out of the corner of their eyes. Knives occasionally flew off of tables, lights came on, and things inexplicably fell off the wall. Despite these somewhat scary events, Markus still felt that this presence was happy for her. And she was almost positive the presence was Alice, the woman who never really wanted to move out of the upstairs apartment after so many years.

One particular day a new employee named Samantha was washing dishes. Suddenly she felt a presence behind her, and then a cool breeze. The hair stood up on the back of her neck. Although Samantha did not turn around, she felt certain that there was someone behind her. She was quite shaken and did not stay long at the company.

Other employees reported a lot of activity at night after they returned from a catering job, often after midnight. Most of them refused to go upstairs, since the presence felt even stronger up there, but almost all the employees mentioned Alice's name, letting her know that they were there.

Something Classic moved to a new facility better equipped to accommodate their growing business, and Delectables by Holly moved in. Holly McLelland, the owner, has also experienced

Alice. One of the first times she remembers noticing her was when she walked into her business late one night during the Christmas season. It was about three in the morning, and it was very cold, she recalled. "I knew she was there and I talked to her. I'm used to it now and it doesn't bother me at all. In fact, I'm thrilled to death—I think it's good that she is watching over us."

Now every morning when McLelland and her staff arrive, they have to adjust the thermostat. It is always set five to eight degrees cooler than when they left the evening before. "Alice must like it cool," McLelland said. It seems so, since one employee reported seeing Alice, or at least a woman. He looked back over his shoulder and saw her pass behind him, headed toward the thermostat.

Alice likes it cool in Delectables by Holly

In her most recent experience, McLelland was talking on the phone as she entered the building. "I told the person on the phone that I didn't want to be alone in here. Suddenly, I said, 'Someone is upstairs.' The alarms hadn't been tripped, but I could hear someone walking above my head."

Although she doesn't like to be in her business alone at night, McLelland insists Alice is amiable. "I talk to her all the time, and I told her at the beginning that I meant her no harm. We could both live here together." But apparently one owner still likes the house a little cooler than the other. McLelland has to come in and adjust the thermostat each day. "It's part of our morning routine now," she said. "We remember Alice every time we walk in the door."

ROSEDALE

JEFF'S WORK IS NEVER DONE

Most people who live in Charlotte don't even realize that there is a plantation on North Tryon Street, only about five minutes from uptown, but there it is, squeezed between industrial sectors and used car lots. Rosedale, this plantation, once extended to include many of those businesses, or at least the land upon which they sit, totaling over 900 acres at one time.

Built in 1815 by a man named Archibald Frew, Rosedale became one of the homes of the Davidson family, one of the most prominent clans in Mecklenburg County. The town of Davidson is named for them, as well as Davidson College. Many of the plantations in the county were owned or connected by marriage to the Davidsons.

Harriet Elizabeth Davidson married Dr. David Caldwell in 1826, and officially gained ownership of Rosedale in 1830. Her father had owned it up until then. Thus Rosedale became the home of the Caldwells during its greatest period. The house, built in Palladian style with a two-story portico and hand-hewn heart of pine shingles, is a unique example of finery for all to see on North Tryon Street. Once called the Salisbury Road, the lane was then as it is now, a main artery into Charlotte. The road lies

The exterior of Rosedale is restored to its original look, including the bright yellow trim, called Paris yellow, which was available in this area in 1815, the year the house was constructed.

exactly where it always has. Everyone that passed realized that the Caldwells were a family of means–and taste.

Then, of course, we come to the part of the tale that every old southern story comes to–the War Between the States. Mrs. Caldwell had already passed away, along with three of her children, in an Erysipelas (similar to strep throat) epidemic, and Dr. Caldwell died a few years later. So soon after the war arrived, Rosedale passed on to its next generation. Baxter, the oldest son, purchased the shares of the plantation from his siblings, all but from Alice, his also unmarried sister, who came to live with him at Rosedale.

Baxter fought in the war. One of his slaves, Jeff, saved his master's life near the end of the fighting at Rock Hill. So after the war, Baxter gave Jeff some land in the Mallard Creek area. Baxter grew old and so did Jeff. After all of Jeff's family died or moved away, Jeff asked to come back to Rosedale. He did so, and took care of Baxter in his old age.

After suffering a stroke, Baxter found himself confined to a wicker wheelchair that sits on display in the basement area of Rosedale today. Every morning Jeff wheeled Baxter out on the back porch and gave him a shave. From the tales told in the family, Jeff kept the shaving goods in a little cabinet in the corner porch column, a cabinet that looks like it would have been perfect for that purpose.

It's easy to imagine looking over the grass early every morning to see this scene, quiet and peaceful, before the day got started. It was that way until Baxter passed away.

Rosedale is now an historic property, open for numerous school tours each year, as well as public tours every Thursday and Sunday afternoon. There are numerous other gatherings that take place on the site throughout the year. The house is often filled with people much like it once was, but there are still many quiet times at Rosedale, like the early mornings when the staff first arrives and makes their way along the gravel path up to the house. Karen McConnell, one of those staff members, remembers Jeff every morning.

"We always try to keep the shaving cabinet closed because birds have a habit of building nests in it if we don't," she explained. "But every morning when I arrive, the shaving cabinet is open." It could not open with a breeze or other such natural occurrence, because it is in a sheltered position and not on easy hinges. "I like to think it's Jeff, opening the shaving cabinet each morning to shave Baxter. It doesn't bother me at all; I just close it and the next morning close it again." There is never any evidence of anyone opening it, no cold spot nor ghostly voice nor other traditional clue. It is simply opened, as naturally as it always was each morning back when Jeff and Baxter were alive.

Other strange occurrences have happened at Rosedale. One visitor looked out a window and saw a lady in period clothing making her way across the lawn. Another visitor had a more shattering event happen to him. "He seemed very comfortable in the house," one docent recalled, "and he naturally made comments during the tour. When we entered the basement, he immediately went to the far corner and started pacing back and forth with a pained expression on his face. I kept giving the tour,

The old shaving cabinet on the back porch at
Rosedale is mysteriously open every morning.

but since it was just him and his wife as our guests that day, I eventually asked what was bothering him. He asked if there was any way he could get behind that wall, so I took him in the storage room. As soon as he walked to that corner, tears started streaming down his face, and he kept saying, 'I'm so sick.' He said that there was a slave boy that laid here, sick, feeling so scared and lonely. It shook me up as well because it was obvious that he felt something very strong, although I'm not sure if he saw anything."

However, for the most part the other "ghosts" are isolated occurrences. It is Jeff, the slave that cannot put down his work, who makes his presence known on a daily basis. And each morning when the staff arrives, they close the shaving cabinet as simply part of their daily routine, just as they open the shutters and get ready for the tours to begin.

ALEXANDER MICHAEL'S

THE OLD BERRYHILL STORE

Tucked away in the literal shadow of the skyscrapers of uptown is an area of Charlotte known as Fourth Ward. Its streets include 10th, 9th, and Poplar on the north side of Church Street, only a short walk from the central corridors of College and Tryon. Extraordinary Victorian dwellings line the avenues, with little yards holding antique rose bushes, jonquils, and occasionally a sleeping cat.

It is in this historic neighborhood, which of course was once not historic but very new, that Star Mills, a local company that produced grits and mill feed, decided to open a retail store. It sat on the corner of 9th and Pine Streets. However, this history is almost forgotten. By the turn of the century, and really until the 1970s, it was known as the old Berryhill store. A very typical "general store" structure with glass windows across the front, set deep under an overhang, it's easy to imagine a small cooler of Coca-Colas sitting by the door, and a couple of people in cane-back chairs on either side of it.

Ernest Wiley Berryhill, whose grand house still stands on the opposite corner from the store, was known as a gracious and considerate man. He ran and then owned the store that stood as a center for the mostly residential area. E. W. died in 1931 after a two-week illness. His funeral took place in his home where everyone attending could look out the window to the store across the street. He was so much a part of this new community—he must have traversed that short walk between his house and store thousands of times. It isn't hard to imagine that he still occasionally does.

The store was a center for news, community business and commerce for many years. It passed in 1941 from Berryhill hands to become a paint shop, a laundry center, and a few more versions of a grocery store until it stood vacant in 1973. It was not until 1983 that the building was permanently saved from destruction, this time to transform into a restaurant and bar.

Alexander Michael's (named for the first owners) opened in 1983, and it has thrived ever since. The building, with its original hardwood floors and quirky layout, is now once again a center of the revitalized community. Steve Casner, the present owner, has taken special pains to retain the character of the place as much as possible. He has also added touches from Charlotte's past to enhance the atmosphere; he constructed the bar from doors of the old Independence Building, and decorated the walls with classic memorabilia and old photographs, including one of the early store. Renters have occupied the upstairs apartment at times over the years. One patron even told Steve he had been born upstairs, back in the days of the Berryhill store.

But it seems that although the apartment upstairs is no longer rented, there is at least one person that prefers not to leave. "There is definitely something different here," Steve said. "I've never

Alexander Michael's has plenty of seating, even for
the ghostly man who occasionally visits the last booth.

personally seen anything, and have been here late at night a lot, but things I can't explain occasionally do happen."

There is a storeroom and office upstairs. New employees often suddenly declare that they won't return to that part of the structure alone. "A lot of my employees in the past have been creeped out by upstairs, saying that they just don't like it up there."

Alexander Michael's houses two original coolers from its days as the Berryhill store, and these sometimes inexplicably open, even though they have fastened latches and a secure seal. "I'll be working down here, usually alone, and hear the coolers pop open behind me, or something like that," Steve said. "But I never really felt that weird about it. It just happens."

Steve admits that some people have had more concrete supernatural experiences in the restaurant. A few years ago, one of the cooks was in early one morning, making coffee and getting ready for the busy day ahead (Alexander Michael's is a favorite for a quick business lunch). The cook walked downstairs and saw a man seated in the last booth. The man wore old-fashioned clothes, including a bowtie, and sat staring straight ahead. When the startled cook stopped, the figure in the booth turned and smiled at him. The man got up and walked toward the door, but disappeared before he reached it; his figure dematerialized, leaving the cook staring at the morning sun streaming through the windows.

Could it be E. W. Berryhill, walking out the familiar door to his home across the street? Or could it be an earlier owner, Andrew Beattie, who died in 1911 of "congestion of the brain?" Beattie's physician said his death was brought on by "work and worry." Could Beattie now be calm enough to smile at an early morning cook? Or could it perhaps be a patron of the store who has come back to see what all the commotion is about?

Whoever it was, and is, Steve Casner said that the presence is all right with him. "I've enjoyed it here, and I've never felt anything bad here. It's always been a place to meet and a center of the community, and I'm glad it's still like that."

OAKLAWN

GHOSTLY HANDPRINTS ON THE GLASS

Oaklawn used to make a beautiful country landscape for those driving past it on McCoy Road in Huntersville. Built in 1821 by Benjamin Davidson (called "Independence Ben" by his family because he was born on May 20, the date of the Mecklenburg County Declaration of Independence), it used to be surrounded by farmland on all sides. Now, however, it almost disappears from the landscape because the housing development of Cedarfield surrounds it. Still, amidst these track homes sits an elegant plantation dwelling with the original smokehouse and well house behind.

The legend goes that Oaklawn is one of the most haunted houses in the county with three ghosts: an old man who shoots a shotgun, a young woman who cries, and a child who is mischievous. Although the present owners have not seen or heard any evidence from the old man, the other two stories appear to be true. Of course, after reading this book you'll realize that there are places in Mecklenburg County that have many more ghosts than two, but I doubt you will find a spirit more disconcerting than the child ghost at Oaklawn, if simply for its determined presence.

The original mistress of Oaklawn was Betsy Latta Davidson Reid, obviously one of the most well-connected people in the county in 1821, since she was related to three prominent families by either birth or marriage. One of the children of James Latta of Latta Plantation, she married Independence Ben, and then after his death in 1829, married Rufus Reid, owner of a plantation called Mount Mourne outside of Davidson. Since Betsy was an avid gardener and Presbyterian, Oaklawn was said to be a unique place under her guidance, with beautiful gardens and slaves that had Sunday off for a day of rest.

After her death and the Civil War, John Moore purchased the estate on the courthouse steps in 1886. It is this family that we think possibly holds the key to identifying the child who refuses

Oaklawn

to leave Oaklawn, since the Davidsons had no children to die young. Unfortunately the child's name has been lost with time.

Mrs. Carol Sadoff, one of the current owners of Oaklawn, loves her home immensely and is a wonderful caretaker of it. Although not connected to the original family, she is very interested in the house's history and preservation. She and her husband Martin purchased the property from the Historic Landmarks Commission in 1994, and were told then that the house was supposedly haunted. "I asked what kind of a ghost it was," Carol recalled. "When I found out it was a child ghost, I thought, 'Well, we can handle that.'" So the couple moved in, and after a few months, Carol's mother, Sophie Goldfarb, also came to live with them.

The activity of the house seems to be centered around an upstairs bedroom. Originally there was one large bedroom, but it was later divided into two rooms. A full bath attaches to one of the bedrooms, the one where Carol and her husband spent their first nights in the home.

"I woke up because I sensed someone in the bedroom," she said. "I saw a shadow by the fireplace, about the size of a child, and I tried to wake my husband up. He said it was my imagination and wasn't concerned, so I just kept staring at it. A green aura started to come around it, and I definitely saw it. I laid there watching it until the sun came up, a couple hours at least. I didn't want to let it out of my sight."

She never saw the figure more defined, and it never moved, but she said she felt it was definitely taking notice of her. "We had been told that the ghost in the house was a little boy who had died of scarlet fever," she explained. The Davidsons never had a child die in the house, but the Moores could possibly have had one that died very young. Carol said it is this presence that is at Oaklawn without a doubt—and not just because of that night when she watched the shadow.

"For a few months after we moved in, whenever we would take a shower in that bathroom and the window would fog up with steam, there would be a small handprint that appeared on the same pane of one window," Sadoff said. "I wiped it off, and it would always come back. It was a small hand and the fingers and all could fit inside the palm of my hand. After a few months, it went away."

They've also heard crying upstairs that they said could be a child or a very sad woman. This was especially audible when the couple sat in the living room, a very formal room near the front door. "We always thought it was the child, but it could be a woman. We're not sure."

It was Mrs. Goldfarb who had the most chilling experience in the house. On her first night sleeping there, she felt someone tickling her feet. She called out, "Who's there?" but heard nothing in response. Upon telling Carol the next morning, they both realized that she sleeps without her hearing aids and could not have heard something if "it" responded. This incident occurred in the very room where Carol saw the shadow by the fireplace and the handprint on the window.

The next night Mrs. Goldfarb stated out loud that if anything happened again, she was not going to stay in the house. It never did, and now she enjoys the home as much as her daughter.

Most of the occurrences happened in the first two years the Sadoffs lived in the residence, and that seems to be a common pattern for some ghosts–a "checking the new owners out" as it were. However, Carol said that some things are still unsettling about the house. Original trees still stand beside the structure, and often over two hundred large crows sit in those trees, almost obliterating the leaves. Crows, long hated in folklore, are often a sign of death or haunting. It appears that at Oaklawn they feel quite comfortable.

CAROLINA THEATRE

GHOSTS IN THE BALCONY

For a place that is less than one hundred years old, the Carolina Theatre on Sixth Street in downtown Charlotte has really been through a lot. Opened in 1927, it has served as the venue for some of showbiz's biggest acts–and biggest movies as well. Charlotte has always known it was a treasure, and a few years ago it was briefly listed on the National Register of Historic Places–until big business tore down its lobby and it was deemed no longer appropriate for the list.

Built as a palace that sold "a theatre experience" instead of just movies, the Carolina offered a Spanish motif, velvet curtains from France, and a luxurious lobby area. Bob Hope, Ethel Barrymore, and Elvis Presley all performed here, and movies such as *Gone with the Wind* first ran here in all their splendor. The Carolina is listed as one of the "Great American Movie Theaters."

Even in its present condition, which some would call rundown, others unrestored, and still others perfect the way it is, the theater has recently served as a unique venue for new and innovative entertainment. The Moving Poets Dance Troupe has used the stage to perform spectacular pieces, including *Dracula* and *Salome.*

The Carolina Theatre as it appeared in 1946
Courtesy of the Charlotte Mecklenburg Historic Landmarks Commission

However, once again big business is having a say in the future of the Carolina Theatre, and once again it currently stands empty.

Bill Freeman, an effects and lighting technician who has worked extensively in the theater over the past few years, says that although there are no performances going on, there is still activity there. In fact, he calls the Carolina Theatre "a little tea party with all sorts of guests."

One guest that Freeman has come in contact with on a number of occasions is someone whom he calls Fred. "One day, I put up a union sticker in the projection booth, the same union that most of the people that worked here belonged to. I began to feel a strong impression of someone in the room, and then the name just popped into my head. That kind of thing doesn't really happen to me, so I guessed that the ghost's name was Fred, and I've called him that ever since."

Fred can be mischievous, almost to the point of ruining a show. Freeman and other technicians have experienced lights inexplicably going off and then turning back on. Things that the technicians had fixed the night before turned up broken again the next night. A couple of times they've had to tell Fred to "knock it off." "Amazingly, the lights will come back on with no explanation," Freeman said. "Things will start working again."

Freeman believes that the presence he saw one day in the balcony was Fred. "He was standing up there, just as if he was watching a show, and he stepped back into the shadows. It was in the lower part of the balcony, and he looked solid, a white man, thirty to forty-ish, in a white oxford shirt." The lights were not on up there, but his form picked up the reflection of light from the stage—that is, until it vanished.

In addition to actually seeing someone, Freeman has also felt cold spots throughout the building. There is one, he said, up in the projection room that seems nice. It's probably the presence of Fred. However, there is another cold spot where Freeman gets the impression of an old lady in dated clothing. And there is another place, a trapdoor near the old orchestra pit, where there "is a very unwelcome feeling," he said. "It feels like it could be the ghost of an unhappy musician. There were a lot of hostilities about using canned music when they changed from a live orchestra because many musicians lost their jobs. I don't like being in that area of the theater." In that particular location, Freeman has experienced a tightness in his chest and general sense of ill will.

Because of these various instances, most actors and technicians pay their respects to the spirits in the Carolina Theatre, often saying goodnight before leaving an empty house. That appears to be a general tradition for those in the theater, not just those who have worked in the Carolina.

Freeman said that he never feels completely alone in the building. "It's a common occurrence to hear seats moving in the balcony or footsteps in another part of the house, but I don't feel threatened or uneasy. I remember the people who were here." Walking in the Carolina Theatre, it's hard to forget history—especially when it is messing with the lights.

The interior of the Carolina in 1946
Courtesy of the Charlotte-Mecklenburg Historic Landmarks Commission

LATTA PLANTATION

FOOTSTEPS WITH NO OWNERS

The most prominent families built their plantations and holdings in northern Mecklenburg County. One such person was James Latta, who came from Ireland to America in 1785. He was a traveling merchant and planter. Latta Plantation, located on Sample Road in Latta Plantation Park, has a long history, and some say that past inhabitants still lurk about the premises, checking up on the property.

In 1799 James Latta paid Moses Hays $600 to purchase a one-hundred-acre tract on the east side of the Catawba River. Latta had been living in nearby Lincoln County. Historians believe he built the Latta House about 1800. In a sparsely populated county, James Latta became a prominent figure. He had three daughters who were educated at Salem Academy (then a boarding school for girls, now a women's college in Winston-Salem, North Carolina). His daughters became the mistresses of some of the finest plantations in the area—Oaklawn, Cedar Grove, and Mount Mourne.

The Latta House held much sorrow throughout its life. The elder Lattas outlived all of their children except one. That daughter lived only a few months longer than her parents, and died during childbirth. One Latta son, Ezekiel, died at the age of ten, while away at school. The parents sadly laid his little body out in the home. During the ante-bellum period, mortality rates were far higher in young people since there was no knowledge of germs and bacteria. Still, we cannot deny the grief of parents losing their children. Just because our ancestors were often surrounded by death does not mean that their grieving was any less.

Today, peaceful and quiet Latta Plantation is a wonderful place to visit, with the river gliding silently beside it. The house is a beautiful structure, elegant in its perfect simplicity, and we are fortunate it has survived along with some of its original outbuildings. Tours are performed on a regular basis. Latta has some animals in the barns and chicken coops. The house is a rectangular two-story frame dwelling covered with beaded weatherboards, and resting on a low stone foundation. It is now surrounded by a green lawn, but it most assuredly was once a bustling place with chickens roaming the grounds, and people coming in and out of the house and working close by.

Latta still has people who work diligently for her. One person who volunteered for many years, Betty Pierce, has always felt a welcoming when coming onto the property. Maybe it's because of the serene beauty, or maybe it's because her family is connected in the region, or maybe it's because *someone* is welcoming her.

Pierce has heard various noises while in the house alone, but the most distinguishable were the footsteps. On at least two occasions she's heard heavy footfalls, but when she looked up, she saw no one. "Once," she recalled, "I was in the dining room, and

Latta Plantation

I heard the back door open—it was locked—and I heard someone walk in. I turned and no one was there and the door wasn't open.

"Another time I was filling in a crack in the wall, and I heard the door open and footsteps again, of course to see no one. It always happened when I was doing something to the house, and I always felt like it was James Latta. Maybe he didn't want me messing with his house, or maybe he was checking up on things. But I never felt scared or anything—it was always a wonderful place to be."

Board president Elizabeth Myers has also had what she calls "experiences" in the house, including a complicated gate latching behind her. But one experience she had with a tour group to bear witness. "I was giving a tour one Christmas Eve, and while downstairs, I heard the attic door slam open," she said. "I looked at everyone and they had heard it too. I just laughed and went on. I moved to another part of the house, and suddenly we heard children running across the garret above us, laughing. Once again, everyone in the group heard it."

Running across the garret is impossible today, for there are obstacles that prevent anyone from passing through it. She said that everyone was amazed, but that she felt like it was some of the Latta children, excited about Christmas.

Another docent at the site encountered something while giving a tour. In one of the rooms, there stands a walking stick owned by the family. At the exact moment this docent mentioned the walking stick, it performed as if on command, and wobbled across the floor before falling some distance away from the wall.

Such tales always get associated with a property as old as Latta Plantation. A generation ago it served as a camping site for Boy Scouts, infamous for their campfire stories. However these are accounts, first-hand, by people who actually experienced them. "Whatever it is," Pierce said, "I've always felt it was James Latta. Whenever we would hear something, I would say, 'Oh, it's just James Latta.'"

Make sure and greet him the next time you visit his home; he'll be watching you even if you don't see him.

311 EAST BOULEVARD

THE BOARDING HOUSE OF DILWORTH

When you ask Charlotte residents if they know of any ghost stories, they mention 311 East Boulevard more frequently than any other location. Situated in historic Dilworth, the one-time boarding house has been the site for some fine Charlotte restaurants throughout the years, including Eli's, Morel's, and Castaldi's. It stands as a city landmark, with the quiet beauty of its architecture just one of many jewels on East Boulevard.

Built in 1900, the house's most famous boarder was Carson McCullers. The highly acclaimed southern author wrote part of her novel, *The Heart is a Lonely Hunter*, in one of the front rooms. An historical plaque outside the restaurant commemorates this. McCullers established her reputation with this novel, her first, a sad tale about loneliness and the outcasts of society. Much of the story takes place in a boarding house. It's hard to imagine East Boulevard as lonely, since the street is a main artery of the city from downtown to Myers Park. In McCullers' day, Dilworth was a quiet suburb, with streets that could often feel lonely, especially to an outsider.

However, although her husband Reeves committed suicide a few years later, it was in Paris and not in Charlotte that McCullers

311 East Boulevard

experienced the loneliness she wrote about, and the ghosts that haunt 311 East Boulevard appear to have nothing to do with the author or her husband except a shared location.

"Sensitives," people who claim to be able to "feel" ghosts, do believe that one is a man who committed suicide in the building, and that his spirit is trapped in the place. There may be another presence as well, this one possibly a woman, but as of yet, no one has seen either of these entities appear as apparitions. Nonetheless, other things have pointed to unexplained presences.

One of the former managers at Castaldi's, Magdi Abdelal, told of an upstairs toilet that flushes by itself. "That scared the hell out of me," she said. Running water and lights are classic ghost "props." (Just think of any movie about hauntings you've ever seen; many of the horrors in those movies start with flushing toilets and running water when no one is around.) Other members of the kitchen and wait staffs have reported objects flying across the kitchen, even a full glass of iced tea smashing against a wall and shattering. Footsteps and loud noises have been reported coming from the stairwell, and a general feeling of "creepiness" has come over many of the staff after the last dinner guests leave for the evening.

Perhaps the most disconcerting event at this Charlotte landmark happened to Bill Knight, owner of Morel's. He came in one day and found the door to an attic closet kicked or forced open from the inside, even though it had been nailed shut. Something on the inside tried and succeeded in getting out, but Knight never saw what it was and had no explanation. That closet wasn't used anymore.

Present tenants are reluctant to discuss their experiences, but with such a long history of the unexplained, one can only imagine that their employees are experiencing much of the same thing. The paranormal seems to be the normal at 311 East Boulevard. After a quick walk around the rambling old place, it's easy to imagine why.

35TH STREET HOUSE

VIOLENT MANIFESTATIONS

At the corner of Farley and 35th streets in Charlotte stands an unassuming house. It is quite literally a little brick box, only eight hundred square feet or so without a front porch or a garage or any architectural details to speak of. Built in 1950, the house straddles the North Davidson and Plaza-Midwood communities, and has had many owners and inhabitants over its simple life. However, within this small house, not a creepy gothic mansion or one surrounded by Spanish moss dripping off a tree-lined avenue, dwells something so disconcerting and downright scary that it made one of its tenants move out in the middle of the night–and never come back.

The story goes that in this house lived a woman who was estranged from her husband. The man lived in Florida although the two were still married. This woman passed away, and only then did the man decide to come live in the house. He too died a few years later. This sounds like a sad but simple story, although in reality any interrelation between two human beings is always extremely complex. But for the sake of argument, this story was neither shocking nor of seeming importance in the great big world.

However, this story and the people in it became very important to Jacob Hilbert, a sous chef at Patou, who lived in the house until recently. He said it all started with a smell without a source. "It was the smell of rot," he explained, "and it was located in the corner of the living room, a horrible smell that no one could find the cause of." He and his roommates ripped up the carpet and still the smell remained. It remained even after they checked the vents for dead animals or anything else out of the ordinary.

Then came the beginning of what Hilbert called "the next phase." A full-time musician back then (he came to cooking only recently), Hilbert and his friends were listening to a CD which they had cut. They all decided to go into the kitchen, so they turned off the CD and the stereo. As they chatted in the kitchen, they heard the CD player come back on and start playing track 8, a song about Hilbert's recently deceased grandfather. They rushed back into the room and checked the machine for an electrical short. When they found none, they marked the whole thing off as an electronic glitch.

"Then the incidents increased in frequency and intensity," Hilbert said. "It was very organic—like it started slow and just grew and grew." The door to Hilbert's room started being locked from the inside, and when he'd come back about twenty minutes later to try it again, the door would open. He began to have trouble sleeping in the room because he felt an intense feeling of isolation, and he could never get the room warm. Finally, as he lay in the dark, he began to hear a woman crying. The weeping happened with such frequency that he moved to the couch and slept there every night for his remaining time in the house. He also got so annoyed at not being able to get into his room that he removed the knob so that the door could not be locked. There were still times when he couldn't get in.

While this was occurring in Hilbert's bedroom, he and his roommates and friends started to feel an angry presence in the kitchen. It wasn't just a feeling—it often displayed itself quite violently. "All of our mugs and coffee cups were eventually destroyed by this thing," he said. Coffee cups would simply explode while sitting on a counter, or would shatter in the middle of the night. In front of a few people, one even flew across the room and hit so hard that it damaged the wall. This was not the same kind of feeling that Hilbert experienced in his bedroom—this one was much more angry, and often dangerous. "We came home

The house on 35th Street

one time, and there was a coffee cup sitting on a red-hot eye of the stove," he said. "It could have burned the place down. But in general, I thought it happened just like it would have with two people fighting. He throwing things in the kitchen, and she off in the bedroom, crying and depressed."

Doorbells rang wildly with no one at the door, and the pilot light on the heater kept going out. One time, with about ten people watching, one of the spirits definitely made itself known. Hilbert said, "We had some friends over to watch TV, and the way this house is situated, when a car comes down the street at night, often its headlights shine in the window. No big deal, we're used to that. But on this particular night when the headlights shone in the window, all of us suddenly saw the outline of a woman, an older lady, from the side, with a bun in her hair. We all saw it, and it was unmistakable; there was nothing that could have cast a shadow like that. If it hadn't been for those headlights, we wouldn't have seen it at all, but she would've still been there."

Amazingly, through all this Hilbert and his friends continued to live in the little house. But there was one final incident that was the "last straw" for Hilbert. When he and the others first moved in, they found an old rocker left in the attic. Not anything spectacular, just a wooden rocker sitting alone in the dusty attic. They left it there, not thinking much of it at the time. As things began to get really uncomfortable in the house, Hilbert started to see the rocker as the symbol of all their problems. He came to believe that it had belonged to the old woman, and that it was important to the house, maybe even the link to whatever was happening to all of them.

So one night when he was at work, he and a friend decided to go home and destroy the rocker. They planned to take it out of the attic and burn it in the backyard. They told no one, and decided to go home immediately after their shifts and take care of it. All went as planned until they entered the attic to get the rocker. It was not there! They knew they hadn't just dreamed the rocker because their friends knew about it. More importantly, they could see the dust-free lines on the floor where the chair's rockers had set. So it had been moved quite recently.

Hilbert and his roommates moved out that night. They understood that it, whatever it was, knew they had planned to get rid of the chair—and it. They decided to leave the situation. They moved a few doors down, told their landlord, and he cut off the electricity to the house. Hilbert and his roommates thought the nightmare was over.

Except when they went back a few days later to get the remainder of their things, the house was dark and very cold—and not happy to see them. "We were more afraid then than we had ever been," Hilbert said. "We took flashlights and entered the house, but our flashlights would not work, only giving us a little pinpoint of light, not spreading out like they normally do. It was literally like the dark was liquid and had form, and we could hear all sorts of things around us, things moving, voices, all kinds of things. We were getting what we needed as fast as we could, and we got the hell out of there."

A new family lives in the house now, and Hilbert said that he hasn't discussed this with them. "They have children, so I don't want to scare them. Maybe it just happened with us and won't happen with everyone who lives there. But actually, they mentioned they are starting to smell a strange smell in the living room."

HOSKINS MILL HOUSE

GHOST IN THE KITCHEN

There is a common story in Mecklenburg County and, for that matter, in the entire southern Piedmont region; the early twentieth century saw a large number of communities spring up and flourish because of the textile mill industry. Chadwick, now called Hoskins, was one such community.

Once an actual suburb of Charlotte, Chadwick was three miles northwest of the city. Of course, Charlotte long ago swallowed up the community into its city limits, but back in its early days Chadwick was responsible for an immediate thirty percent increase in the county's industrial capacity when it opened its textile mills. At one time 1,600 people worked in those mills, and all those people needed a place to live.

Enter the "mill village," a fixture of Mecklenburg County and the South. Countless houses, most constructed with similar floor plans, lined the streets surrounding the mills. The employees could simply walk home in the evenings, around the bend or up the hill to their waiting family on the porch.

One such house in the Hoskins Mill district is now owned by Bobby Lance. Urban renewal has not yet taken hold in this section as it is beginning to in the North Davidson Mill district, or

The great building at Hoskins Mill, as it looks today

around the former Atherton Mill. These homes are still intact.
Most still face one another with their facades as they have since
they were constructed. Lance's home, built in 1947, seems just
another of these houses until one steps inside. Lance has under-
taken the restoration of the home, and the hardwood floors
gleamed and a cozy fire crackled in the fireplace the day the author
visited.

Although Lance has taken on many home improvements, he
has not been without supervision, for he attests to feeling a strong
presence in the kitchen. Sometimes he witnesses more concrete
evidence that there is someone just as interested in the house as
he is.

A few months after he moved in, a friend was over cooking
dinner, while Lance sat in the adjoining dining room, chatting

over a glass of wine. "All of a sudden, a sheet pan that was leaning against the wall in the dish drainer moved," he recalled. "It flew off the counter and landed a few feet away on the floor. My friend was out the door. It really scared him, and he didn't want to stay in the house a minute longer."

When asked why he thought this occurred, Lance recounted what he knew about the previous owner, and added an impression he got from the kitchen itself. "Well, there was an older lady who lived here who passed away. I think it's her, and that she is real particular about the kitchen. I feel her most of the time in there, and it's almost like she is stuck there."

In fact, there was a former owner, Margaret Honeycutt, who passed away. Her husband, Henry, had died a few years earlier. As these stories go, after his death Margaret spent a lot of time alone in her house, but could it be her who sits up late nights, taking stock of the changes in her home from the kitchen?

During the holidays, Lance had another experience that convinced him there is a presence that still thinks it owns the house. One night he and a friend, Mike Lawson, heard the dogs start growling and barking wildly. Though they are usually sweet dogs, this time they had bared their teeth as they looked into the kitchen. Lawson said, "You could feel the mood of the house. It was very uncomfortable, like something that was angry was moving around the house."

The next night around 10:30, the same thing happened. This time the two men walked into the kitchen and found the air in there unpleasant, with cold spots everywhere. "All of a sudden, I felt her touch me," Lawson said, "and Bobby felt her place her entire hand on his back and almost shove him out of the room." The two were understandably shaken, especially since Lance had felt comfortable in the house for so long, even though he thought it was home to a ghost.

The two asked each other if they had moved anything in the kitchen. Did you change something around? Is there something that was in here that's not now? They realized that a couple of days before they had moved an amaryllis that was in the way, although thriving, in the kitchen. Lance had moved it into the bedroom. There its sturdy stalk had drooped and the leaves broken toward the pot, though it appeared to be getting enough water and sunlight.

They got the amaryllis and placed it back on the kitchen counter. Lawson said, "Immediately the commotion stopped. It was peaceful. When we looked at the amaryllis the next day, it was alive again! The stalk was once again straight and the leaves were perfect."

So Lance has decided that although Mrs. Honeycutt did get a little angry, usually she is a comforting presence. "I never feel scared here," he said. "I think she's okay with things for the most part, and sometimes I feel like she protects me."

And it seems that Lance could need protecting, for he fears there is something loitering in the back corner of his backyard that is not so nice. He explained that a friend visited and told him that something evil was in the backyard. "She is Wicca, and she thought she could handle it, but apparently she invited 'it' in one day."

Above: The Hoskins Mill house, home of Bobby Lance and another resident who prefers to remain unseen

Below: The kitchen of the Hoskins Mill house, the center of the paranormal unrest

On that day, after this friend visited the backyard she came into the living room. Suddenly the Dalmatian lunged at the closed front door. All who were seated there heard a thump. Amazingly, when they opened the door, it was dented from the outside as if something had tried to get in. There was no way that the dog could have made such a dent. Both Lance and his friend thought that it must have been whatever was in the backyard. "She blessed a candle and told me to burn it, and I haven't had any problems with that since." The yard, long and narrow, backs up to railroad tracks and some woods behind what is now a bakery. After dark, it's easy to imagine the yard having a sinister nature, being a place that is perfect for foul deeds.

So why on this small piece of land is there so much activity? Could it be that there is something that prevents spirits from moving on? Perhaps this was a place where such hardworking people came home so many times that there was a build up of energy. There are innumerable stories in a mill village such as Hoskins; this story tells of everyday people living everyday lives, even beyond the grave.

7TH STREET

RUMORS OF SPECTERS

Seventh Street in Charlotte is one where there just ought to be ghosts. The main artery through Elizabeth, one of Charlotte's trendiest neighborhoods, the street is lined with big oak trees and eclectic businesses in buildings that once served as homes for the up-and-coming in the 1920s. The following two stories are unsubstantiated, but are definitely worth a visit. Elizabeth no doubt holds many more stories such as this behind its well-kept front doors.

In the evening when the shadows lengthen, some of the houses take on a sinister look with their facades obscured by large trees or climbing vines. One such house at 1800 East 7th Street has served as the home of one of Charlotte's favorite restaurants since 1985. The Cajun Queen, where you can get great gumbo, hurricanes, and live Dixieland jazz music seven nights a week, has had ghost stories floating around about it for years. It's easy to see why.

Unlike most other restaurants that knock down walls and change the character of a place, the Cajun Queen chose to keep the house intact, including its interesting woodwork and myriad of rooms. This provides an intimate experience for patrons because it really feels like you are dining in the past–not to mention the dark New Orleans' colors that splash the walls or the decadent air about the place. But as restaurants do, the Cajun Queen has had several staff changes over the years, and none of its current employees report anything unusual.

"It's been about ten years since I've heard anything about ghost stories," said Tim, the general manager. "We used to have some employees who claimed they had experienced something in this building, but no one lately has mentioned it." However, there are a few things that point to something "a little strange" happening in the house originally built in 1920.

About ten years ago a kitchen worker named Musa was finishing up his shift. He was in the basement, a dark, windowless

Cajun Queen

cavern that houses the ice machine and the offices. "From what I remember," Tim recalled, "Musa said that the ice machine spit out ice like it was possessed. Nothing was really going on; all of a sudden ice just started flying out of the machine." A malfunction? Perhaps.

What also keeps people talking is a tradition that the band follows. Doug Henry, longtime band member explained: "When we sing a birthday song in this house, your wish comes true. I say that the ghost upstairs in the attic has something to do with it, but I've never personally had anything happen in the house. I just say it because this guy who used to be in the band started saying it. That's all."

Just down the street from the Cajun Queen is a park at the corner of Hawthorne and 7th. Independence Park is often filled with neighborhood get-togethers and people relaxing or playing Frisbee, just like any other park, but its unusual shape and size make it stand out. It sits lower than street level, and extends only a block with no nature trails or other modern equipment save the children's playground. This was Charlotte's first public park, spearheaded by D. A. Tomkins, and it underwent numerous changes throughout the years, including the additions of Memorial Stadium at one end, Park Center, a now vanished rose garden, and the Arhelger Memorial. The ghost story of Independence Park centers on the last edifice.

Lillian Arhelger was a vibrant twenty-one-year-old from Texas who had just completed her first year as coach of the Central High School women's basketball team. In June of 1931, she accompanied the Girl Scouts from Myers Park Presbyterian Church on a

The Arhelger Memorial in Independence Park

field trip to Blowing Rock, North Carolina and Glen Burnie Falls. An excerpt from the Charlotte Landmarks Commission files best explains what happened next:

> The girls bolt along the path to the top of the falls and leap onto the perilous rocks that border the precipice. Then disaster strikes. "Virginia is going over the falls," her playmates scream. Lillian does not hesitate. She jumps into the swirling water and gropes for the hand of the desperate child. It's too late. They both careen sixty feet downward into the deluge of the Glen Bernie [sic] Falls.
> The child survives. Lillian lies crumpled on the other side of the river. Her skull is fractured. Pieces of a decayed log protrude from her mouth and nose. Somehow as if to atone for the tragedy, the children and the counselors hold vigil on the lawn of the Blowing Rock Episcopal Church, where Lillian's limp and unconscious body waits for the ambulance. Lil-

lian Arhelger died the next day in Lenoir, N.C., never having come out of a coma.

Her death stunned the students of Central High School, who had lost one of their brightest teachers and coaches. So they started a campaign that raised $1,000 in just three weeks to erect a memorial to the woman who had been so brave. It still stands today in Independence Park, largely the same as it was when unveiled.

And the ghost that haunts Independence Park? Why, Lillian Arhelger, of course. Her transparent form, clothed in white, looks for the little girl that she never knew she saved. She haunts the park because it is there that she is remembered. Generations of children pass on her brave death tale, and then dare one another to wait for the ghost to appear around dusk.

Lillian Arhelger

QUEENS COLLEGE

MRS. BURWELL FEELS AT HOME

Queens College has been an institution in Charlotte since the mid part of the nineteenth century. Until recently an all-girls college, it was the sister institution of its Presbyterian brother school in the northern part of the county, Davidson College. Located on Selwyn Avenue, Queens looks like a classic small college campus, complete with large trees, brick buildings covered in ivy, and of course a ghost story or two.

One of the most widely known and documented stories is that of Margaret Anna Burwell. One of the founders of Queens College, she was known to possess a strong personality in life, and it seems, after. Mildred Morse McEwen, an alumnus of Queens as well as a professor of chemistry there from 1924 until 1971, wrote a history of the school, *Queens College, Yesterday and Today*. In it, she explains not only how the Burwells started the school, but also the type of person she was:

The Reverend Robert Burwell and his wife, Margaret Anna Burwell (wife, mother, educator), came to Charlotte and opened the school in the fall of 1857. Since 1837 they had operated "Burwell's Female School" in Hillsborough, North Carolina where Dr. Burwell has also been pastor of the Presbyterian Church. Dr. Burwell is listed in catalogs of that time as Principal of the Charlotte Female Institute [Queens' original name] but Mrs. Burwell was obviously the "power behind the throne;" it was she who stated and administered the rules. (30)

Mrs. Burwell was known as a handsome woman at the time, "and she was nearly six feet tall. In a family history her eldest son, John Bott Burwell, wrote that industry was a prominent trait of her character, and that she had 'unbounded energy and perseverance.'" (31) That makes sense because she persistently attempts to make her presence known to employees of the college.

Mrs. Burwell is said to roam about Burwell Hall, now an administrative building, but one that used to hold the library on its second floor. She appears very solid and real, except for two things that give away she's a spirit—she is obviously dressed in period clothes, and those who see her cannot hear any movements. Although no one I talked with has seen her, many are convinced that she does still inhabit the building.

"She keeps the furnace stoked at night because I can hear the clanging of the pipes all up and down the building," Winnie Bryce, CAS Admissions Office Manager, said. "It's usually late after most people have left, and I can hear things. Still, I feel like she is a good ghost."

Eileen Dills, Dean of CAS Admissions, said, "Many times when I'm alone in my office at night, I hear the door to my office bathroom begin to creak, and it opens by itself. Sometimes when I'm sitting at my desk, I can hear the door open and I don't look around, I just keep working." Could it be just the quirks of an old building, perhaps an uneven floor? Dills does not think so. "Sometimes I can see the knob turn before it opens."

The October 1999 issue of *Royal Focus*, the Queens College newsletter, reported that Mrs. Burwell makes "her presence known by opening desk drawers, clanging on pipes, opening doors and taking joy rides in the building's elevator." (1) The staffs of the President's Office and the Office of Institutional Advancement have also reported desk drawers and file cabinets opening by themselves. Tamara Leavell said about a drawer, "Once I swear I had it locked, and it opened by itself."

The *Royal Focus* also reported:

> Other buildings around campus are said to have haunts of their own. Students living in the residence halls have seen and heard some strange things. Some former students who used to live in Harris Hall have had ghost sightings. One student said he woke up in the middle of the night and saw what looked like an older woman dressed in old

Burwell Hall

Margaret Anna Burwell
From *Queens College: Yesterday and Today*

clothing, hovering over his bed. He was so scared that for the rest of the year he slept with his overhead light on. A former student in Albright Hall said the stations on her stereo used to change mysteriously, and the same thing happened to the stereo of the next resident who lived in her room. (1)

In the past few years, Queens College has launched a successful night school for non-traditional students wishing to earn undergraduate and graduate degrees after work. Many people, people not overly familiar with the campus, attend class after dark. One can only wonder what happens to students who get lost trying to find their classrooms. Does a six-foot-tall tour guide with gray curls framing her face ever help them find the way?

RAILROAD TALES

TANKTOWN AND NORTH DAVIDSON

Railroads have been a backbone of the South for a long time. They have brought us industry, knowledge of other places, and have become a symbol of the South and all rural America. Many southern writers have used railroads in their work, including the creator of "Southern" for a lot of Americans, Tennessee Williams. He often used them as symbols of loneliness and a wish for something more.

Ghost stories quickly started cropping up about railroads—spirits who walked the track, lonely disembodied (or dismachined?) whistles, and even phantom trains that flew out of the mist and scared a driver who was crossing the track. As an area of trains, tracks, and a center of industry for the region, Mecklenburg County has its share of railroad ghosts and superstitions, including the ones that come out of Tanktown (now Crestdale) in Matthews, and the mill village of North Davidson.

Matthews is one of the small towns in a county dominated by the large metropolis of Charlotte. Now a bedroom community for many of Charlotte's employees, Matthews was once a thriving center on its own, fueled by the railroad. At the eastern border of the community, spanning both sides of the railroad, was Tanktown, Matthews' African-American section. The name "Tank-town" referred to the railroad water tank that originally stood at the heart of the district, near the tracks. The men who operated the tank and lived nearby made up the community's earliest residents. From its settlement, African-American men and women traversed between this district and the greater town of Matthews, working an assortment of jobs, for as in most of the South, they provided much of the backbone of the area's work-force.

The quickest route from Tanktown into Matthews proper was parallel to the railroad tracks down Charles Street. Caldwell Russell, lifetime resident of Matthews, recalled, "A lot of people would walk the tracks on their way to and from work." One of those people, Lulabelle Caldwell, worked for his family for many years as a domestic. "Every night if it was getting late, she would say, 'Got to get home before the chain come up.' She came to work for us in 1936, so this story must have been well established before then."

It seems that a young man was on his way to work early one morning, walking the tracks. A train hit and killed him. The news rippled through Tanktown, and it wasn't long after that people in the community started to worry about the supernatural conse-quences of the accident.

The story goes that if you passed by a particular spot on that railroad track at midnight, a chain would rise up and block your path. From the way that Russell described the story, one can only imagine a long chain snaking its way out of the ground, going straight up, and then stretching itself along the track, suspended

Residents of Matthews' Tanktown used to walk these tracks
to and from work—until midnight when "the chain came up."

in the air. You could not get around it, and didn't want to even think about trying. The story stopped there.

"From the way she told it," Russell said, "I assumed that she was talking about an actual linked chain blocking her path. She was serious about it and worried that she wouldn't make it home in time." As for if this tale was ever tested, it seems that all were too terrified to venture out, or perhaps too terrified to recall it if they did. The reason for associating a chain with the man's death has been lost to time, but it makes quite an unusual story—a ghost chain.

The next railroad tale comes from deeper in the heart of Mecklenburg County. North Charlotte, as it was known, was the mill community that surrounded Highland Park Manufacturing Company Mill No. 3. Depending on whom you asked, the community had differing reputations. For some people it was a notorious part of town where it was easy to get into trouble, for others it was a great place to grow up, and for others it was simply a place to come home after a hard day's work in the mill. The Charlotte Historic Landmarks Commission explains the details:

> Originally eighty mill houses, white frame dwellings in several blocks of neat rows across from the mill, were built, and more were added later. A quarter of a mile up the extension of Brevard Street another mill was being put up in 1904, the Mecklenburg (later Mercury), and eventually a third (Johnson Manufacturing Co., 1913) was built between the first two, both of which also had their own areas of mill houses. The North Charlotte community thrived for many years, complete with hotel, a mercantile business with stores and lodge rooms above, and drug and grocery stores.

The railroad brought cotton to the manufacturing plant and took goods away for distribution. Highland was a large producer of ginghams in its heyday (it closed in 1965), so the track was a central artery for the community. One very visible reminder of the rail was what was known as the North Charlotte trestle. It was on Heron Avenue, and it went over the Mill Pond, where, incidentally, at the time of this writing, was the exact location for a condo construction site.

There are two stories associated with this spot. The first underwent testing by many a group of young boys daring one another. In the early part of the twentieth century, a man swinging a lantern, looking for something on the track or perhaps working somehow for the railroad, was killed by a train one night. Jesse Atkins, who grew up in North Charlotte, explained: "When I was a kid, people said that you could hear music out there, and it was supposed to be that man that was killed." It was like the tinkering of bells or perhaps chimes. Sometimes it went with a mysterious light bobbing about the track. Young boys strained their ears to hear the music, and some reported that they did.

Another more gruesome event happened at the same location in the 1950s. A young man rode in the back of his father's pick up truck. As they approached the North Charlotte trestle, the boy stood up to look down Heron Avenue. He didn't realize they were so close to the low bridge as he was facing the opposite direction. The trestle decapitated him. Atkins said not long after this occurred, the story began to circulate that the boy walked the track, wandering aimlessly. Atkins said that he never saw the boy.

One thing that is interesting about these two stories is that they both are linked to persons who came in direct contact with the railroad–one killed by a bridge and the other by an actual train. This illustrates the virtual personification of the railroad as a living entity, able to shape destinies. And it lays the groundwork for those phantom train stories–they are more than just machines.

POPLAR AND SEVENTH

BOOTLEGGER'S FOOTPRINTS

In big cities things get knocked down. New buildings are built over the architectural footprints of old ones, and soon no one can remember what it used to be. Such is the case with First Ward, a revitalizing neighborhood in downtown Charlotte. Collective memories being what they are, we can only now recall it as the former site of Earle Village. The public housing is now demolished and gone, and something new is in its place, but even before that, First Ward was once a "good address" (and people are trying to make it so again), a bustling community with churches, schools, and beautiful Victorian homes.

It is one such home, originally situated at 225 Caldwell Street, that now is of interest. It was one of the houses saved years ago, and moved precariously through downtown to other parts of the city. The home at 225 Caldwell literally landed on a plot at 400 North Poplar Street, in the beautiful and *Southern Living*-famous Fourth Ward.

Now owned by Randy Cernohorsky and John Causby, the house has seen substantial renovation. "We have done a lot of work on it," Cernohorsky said, "from literally shoring up the floor to a new roof to a new water heater." But of course this book is not about home renovations. It's about ghosts.

Cernohorsky said, "The lady we purchased the house from told us at closing that we had a ghost. We didn't think that much about it at the time, but there have been some things that definitely cannot be explained easily here." From the information the former owner passed on, this ghost is supposedly that of a boot-legger who used to own the house.

He used to sell his alcohol in the front hall. People often walked up on the porch "to visit for a spell," so he must have seemed a popular man to his First Ward neighbors. If the visitors were not buyers, he kept the liquor hidden from sight behind a secret trap door under the stairs in the front hall. And from the type of haunting, this man must have had a good business go-ing—he needs a lot of water, and of course making alcohol requires lots of water.

"The first thing that happened" Cernohorsky recalled, "was a few months after we moved in. In the middle of the night, the faucets came on in the upstairs bath. You could hear it come on, and when we checked, they were running." After he turned the water off, nothing else happened for some time.

"Then I came downstairs one morning to make coffee a while after that, and I didn't see or hear anything. When my roommate came down the stairs, he saw puddles on each step, like someone had just walked down the stairs barefoot after stepping in water. We couldn't figure out where the water came from; it wasn't raining, there were no leaks anywhere, and I had on shoes that were dry. I was standing in the kitchen the whole time and I didn't

The house at Poplar and Seventh

hear anything like someone walking down the stairs, but the water was there."

Guests have routinely reported the feeling of being watched. On occasion there are noises upstairs when no one is up there, but Cernohorsky quickly explained, "We have a creaky attic with lots of stuff up there, and I'm sure that's just an old house creaking." One guest, Cynthia Mann, reported that she saw a lady in her room late one night, and refused to sleep in that room ever again.

One night when neighbors Fred and Jeannie Taylor were at the house for dinner, they felt someone pass by them. Cernohorsky said, "They were in separate rooms, and almost at the same time they both stopped and walked into the hallway to see each other. 'Did you just feel that?' they both asked each other, and they had distinctly felt someone pass by them but had not seen anything."

The owners of the home have never felt anything similar, but they do report some strange happenings. The den, a central room of the house, is always cold, and the heating and cooling systems work sporadically. They have a cat, and she often backs into a corner of the hallway and screeches, reacting to something at the front door, when there is nothing there. And then there was the chair incident.

"I don't know if it was a ghost," Cernohorsky explained, "but one time we came home and one dining room chair was moved. It was actually on two legs. One leg was propped precariously on a leg of the table. It could have been the cat, but that had never happened and hasn't happened since." Could it have been the bootlegger, startled from calculating his books in the dining area adjacent to the front hall?

Cernohorsky is slow to acknowledge that it is the ghost. With all the structural movement that has happened to the house, including the fact that it doesn't sit on its original site, some would doubt this ghost's existence. Except how can you attribute faucets turning on and wet footsteps to the simple creaking of an old house?

STUDIO EAST

BROTHER RALPH PLAYS ON

Arthur Smith is a Charlotte legend. The musical and radio and television personality was responsible for one of the best-known "Southern" songs, "Dueling Banjos." This story revolves around him and the legacy of music he helped found in this region.

The career of Arthur Smith as a recording artist began with RCA in 1936. Later, he and Bob Wills were the first two Country Music artists to sign with MGM in the mid-forties. Arthur wrote and recorded his first hit record "Guitar Boogie" in 1945. It became the first instrumental to reach the top of the Country charts, then crossover and reach the top of the Pop charts. In 1955 Arthur wrote and recorded a tune entitled "Feuding Banjos" which was a charted record. However, Warner Bros. renamed and claimed it as a traditional adaptation in 1973 as the theme for the motion picture *Deliverance*. "Dueling Banjos" was BMI's Song of the Year in 1973. Arthur sued Warner Bros. and won a landmark infringement case in Federal Court in New York.

He also created, produced, and marketed the first Country Music-oriented television show to be syndicated nationally. "The Arthur Smith Show" ran for an unbroken span of thirty-two years. The list of guest appearances is a Who's Who List of Entertainers,

Studio East

including musical artists of all categories. In addition, his early morning show, "Carolina Calling," ran for a decade in the 1950s and 60s. It was a perennial ratings winner. This daily hour-long variety show featured Arthur Smith and His Cracker-Jacks, Brother Ralph and Cousin Fudd (Tommy Faile), Little Wayne "Skeeter" Haas, and Arthur's Crossroads Quartet. Top Country Music stars, Broadway stars, Hollywood figures, and recording artists from all types of music appeared on the show, as well as sports figures, politicians, and international stars.

Of course, there was the recording studio. On Monroe Road, across the street from Sharon Memorial Park Cemetery, and directly beside a crematorium sits Studio East. An unobtrusive building constructed in 1965, it is easy to miss, even if you're looking for it. The former Arthur Smith Studio moved to this location in the sixties, and many greats have recorded here over the years.

Studio East is relatively small, but has a regional and national clientele that has ranged from John Mellencamp to Randy Travis to James Brown. Owner Tim Eaton said of Studio East, "A lot of people have recorded here, and the history throughout this place has created rumors of a friendly spirit. People say that they see images out of the corner of their eyes, walking past, and when they look up, they're gone."

Rumors and artists' superstitions are somewhat to blame, of course, for the claim that Studio East has a ghostly presence, but the root of the rumor revolves around some very definite occurrences that cannot be explained. One night at about two a.m., a sound technician was leaving after a late recording session. The studio was dark, with no musicians in it, and all the equipment turned off. "The talkback button was hit, something that is not easy to do," Eaton explained. "It's the button where artists in the studio can talk to the booth, and someone said, 'Good night,' to that technician over the speaker."

People who visit and work at Studio East say that "things out of the norm" happen there pretty consistently. Eaton and others associated with the studio have a theory. "The rumors have always been that it's Arthur Smith's brother, Ralph. It's a very friendly spirit, and Ralph was a wonderful person in life. I feel like he is continuing to look over the musical community."

On the television show, Ralph and comedian Tommy Faile were famous for their antics. They would often dress up in various costumes and perform skits, and both were classic cut-ups. "They

On the set of "Carolina Calling;" from left to right:
Brother Ralph, Lois Atkins, Arthur Smith, and Tommy Faile

were funny, but if you knew Ralph, he was a great personality, a spiritual person." In short, Ralph was full of life.

"If anybody would still be making jokes and having fun," Eaton said, "it would be Tommy and Ralph." And it seems that they are having fun, playing with the studio equipment, roaming the halls, and generally watching over the activities of their old recording location, now Studio East.

Or could there be another explanation, maybe that of restless spirits wandering across the street from the cemetery or next door from the crematorium? If not, Studio East's location nevertheless provides a "comfortable" residence for those who might not have been ready to leave life.

FIRE STATION NO. 4

WHERE THERE'S SMOKE

It was a typical early morning at Firehouse No. 4 on April 1, 1934. Firemen were asleep on their cots in the two-story station on Church Street, when suddenly an alarm came in. One particular fireman, Pruitt Black, was not supposed to be there. He was working a double shift, possibly as a disciplinary action, and he jumped off his cot like everyone else. What happened next made *The Charlotte Observer* the next day:

> When the alarm came in, the firemen, who were sleeping on the second floor of the station, dressed hurriedly and started for the brass pole which leads from the dormitory to the first floor where the apparatus is housed. A fellow fireman said that Black started toward the pole, drawing on his coat as he went. Just as he grasped for the pole, his foot appeared to slip and he missed his catch and fell through the opening. His head struck the concrete below and was horribly smashed. (1A)

Black had been with the fire department for six years at the time of his death. He was twenty-eight years old, and a member of the fire department baseball team. Undoubtedly he had slid down that same pole countless times before he met his death. He was known for smoking cigars, and it's easy to imagine him

Above: Fire Station No. 4
Below: Pruitt Black
From *Charlotte Fire Department: Millennium History 2000*

occasionally sliding down the pole with one clenched in his teeth. However, on that April 1st his time was up.

Members of Box 97 Fire Station on Beatties Ford Road also responded to the call, and they joined their fellow firefighters at Number 4 station. Of course when they arrived, they quickly realized the grave state of Black. A few firemen remained with Black while the others responded to the call. Someone called an ambulance, which took Black to the hospital where he died at 10:45 a.m.

BLACK DROPS FOURTEEN FEET TO HIS DEATH

Loses Footing and Plunges Through Pole Hole.

SKULL IS BADLY CRUSHED

Accident Occurs at Station No. 4 After Alarm; Second Death in Month.

The April 2, 1934
Charlotte Observer

Black was the second fireman from that station to lose his life. Only thirty days earlier, Joe Westnedge died on East Fourth Street while on a call. He too suffered a violent death when he got wedged and crushed between the fire truck and a tree.

Mr. Black apparently does not know exactly what happened that April day in 1934, for he insists on maintaining a residence at Charlotte Fire Station Number 4. The station remained in operation until 1972, when private businesses took over the building. Catwalk, a digital media company, set up offices in the old fire station before moving some years ago to another location on Hamilton Street. Several employees reported "experiences" during their years at No. 4.

"I never specifically saw anything," Susan Cody said, "but I worked there a lot at night by myself and I would feel a presence there. It was never anything definite, but I felt like someone was watching me." Other employees came upon a man in the hallway "that wasn't really there." Many noticed an odor in the building—cigar smoke. Richard Aldridge, Catwalk's owner, said, "No one smoked cigars in there, but many people said that they would all of a sudden smell the scent of cigars."

After Catwalk moved out, another business owner, Mike Lakoff, had more definite experiences that eventually led him to do his own research on the place. The first thing he noticed was what the employees of Catwalk had smelled, the same scent of cigar smoke. "In 1997, I was walking through the building for the first time," Lakoff said. "It had been boarded up and no one in there for years, and my first thought was that someone had been living there because the smell of cigar smoke was so strong. It was consistent and stronger in some areas than others, but I smelled it throughout the entire time I had my business there."

Lakoff opened an antique and art gallery, aptly named, the Old Fire House. He and a crew did some extensive renovation work to the building before it opened. It was during this period of work that Lakoff said things really started to happen.

"One Sunday afternoon, I was working by myself in the building. A Panthers game had just ended, and there were people milling around on Graham Street. It was pouring rain, and I walked down the back staircase to the main garage below. In the front right corner, I saw a man wearing a sort of parka—it was bright yellow—and I assumed (although the doors were locked) that he had somehow come in from the crowd outside. He walked toward a wall and disappeared. Where he disappeared, we later found had been an original door to the outside when the firehouse was built. It was the first time anything definite happened in the house, and I chalked it up to the fact that somehow, people were getting in, or perhaps that there was someone living here that I didn't know about. It unnerved me, and I left for the day."

He continued the work on the building. One day both he and the electrical contractor, Patrick, had such a bizarre experience that Lakoff could no longer deny there was a presence. Patrick was upstairs, working in the long main corridor, when he encountered a man. This man walked down the hallway and went into what was the original firemen's barracks, and where the pole had been—the one that Black had tried to go down the day he died. Patrick followed the man into the old barracks, but when he entered, the man had disappeared.

Immediately after Patrick discovered that the man had vanished, Lakoff, who was working downstairs, saw a figure cross the room and walk out "the door." "The electrical contractor decided that he no longer wanted to work in that building alone at night, and as far as I know, he never saw the figure again."

But soon Lakoff came face to face with the mysterious man. A few days later, the windows were open on the second floor, letting light in, but there was no electricity in the building. "I was walking down that same upstairs corridor, and I saw a figure facing me. I thought it was a reflection until I realized that the windows were just uncovered; there was no glass in them at the time.

"At that moment, I knew it was something else. We didn't make eye contact, but he had on green khaki canvas pants, he had on a hat, although not a fireman's hat, and later I found out that it was the same person that Patrick had seen."

He started to do research. Lakoff said he found out about the tragic accident, and he came across a picture of Pruitt Black. "It was the man I had seen." Throughout the years he worked in that building, from that point on Lakoff said hello and good-bye to Pruitt each day. "We never had any conversations, and I never felt scared. I felt very protected, but I definitely felt there was someone there."

A friend from San Francisco heard the story and sent Lakoff some old fireman's uniforms and equipment. Lakoff kept it in a room originally used for equipment storage. He routinely had to refold it and put it back on the shelf because the door would be open and the uniforms hanging on old pegs used for equipment hanging all those years ago. There were lots of little things like this that soundly convinced Lakoff that his ghost was a fireman—and a specific one at that.

Others encountered the active ghost. During local gallery crawls, revelers could hear pacing upstairs in that hallway, and customers heard someone walking upstairs when no one was there. Many a person commented on the strong scent of cigar smoke. Even Lakoff's pets knew the ghost. "My dog would routinely stare at two places in the building for hours—the patched flooring where the original fire hole was, and the place in the wall where the door had been. The first time I brought him into the place, he immediately went to that door and began sniffing. He never barked or growled or anything; he just stared like he was interested in something."

And then there was a cockatiel. Lakoff got a bird, Sparky, for the shop that would stay there at night. The bird became very attached to him and a few regular customers. When Sparky saw someone he was familiar with, he would start chirping wildly and say, "Hello, hello, hello," over and over. "Well, there was a security system that was voice sensitive. Routinely in the middle of the night, Sparky would start talking and whistling wildly, just like someone came in that he knew very well." Lakoff added with a chuckle, "I was convinced that he was having conversations with Pruitt."

From Lakoff's research, he said that Black was a kind, religious man. He only smoked cigars inside the firehouse, because although he enjoyed them, smoking was seen as un-Christian. However there are many who have voiced speculations that possibly this kind man did not simply have an unfortunate accident. Is Black still hanging around, trying to let us in on the truth, but failing to get his message across?

Whatever, if it is indeed Pruitt Black who haunts the Old Fire Station No. 4, he is definitely pleased with what has occurred there recently. The station is once again being transformed, this time into a Fire Museum. Be sure to visit it and take a whiff when you walk in. Do you smell cigar smoke?

Photo courtesy of David Campbell

Stephanie Burt Williams is a third-generation native Charlottean. She is an Instructor of American Studies at the University of North Carolina at Charlotte, and has previously written for *Carolina Bride, Lake Norman Times, Sanskrit, Parting Gifts,* and *The Hollins Critic.* This is her first book.